Discovering
Cultures

Chile

Dana Meachen Rau

Marshall Cavendish
Benchmark
New York

For Charlie and Allison

With thanks to Peter T. Johnson, Princeton University, for the careful review of this manuscript.

Marshall Cavendish
99 White Plains Road
Tarrytown, New York 10591-9001
www.marshallcavendish.us

Text copyright © 2007 by Marshall Cavendish Corporation
Map and illustrations copyright © 2007 by Marshall Cavendish Corporation

All Internet sites were available and accurate when sent to press.

Library of Congress Cataloging-in-Publication Data

Rau, Dana Meachen, 1971–
Chile / by Dana Meachen Rau.
p. cm. — (Discovering cultures)
Includes bibliographical references and index.
ISBN-13: 978-0-7614-1988-4
ISBN-10: 0-7614-1988-8
1. Chile—Juvenile literature. I. Title. II. Series.
F2208.5.R38 2006
983—dc22   2006011472

Photo Research by Candlepants Incorporated
Cover Photo: Frances Muntada/Corbis

The photographs in this book are used by permission and through the courtesy of; *Corbis*: Robert Van der Hilst, 1; Charles O'Rear, 4(left), 32(top); Julio Donoso, 8(lower); Hubert Stadler, 9, 11(top), 19, 43, (top left), 43(lower left); Reuters, 10(right), 14(top), 43(middle left); Pablo Corral V, 17; Richard T. Nowitz, 24(left), 36(inset); James L. Amos, 25; David Forman; Eye Ubiquitous, 29; Diego Granja/Reuters, 31; BSPI, 33(low); Larry Dale Gordon/zefa, 34; Tony Arruza, 35; Jose Luis Saavedra, 38. *Getty Images*: Skip Brown, 4(right), 42(right); Mathias Clamer, 8(top); David W. Hamilton, 18; MedioImages, 37; 44. *The Image Works*: David Frazier, 10(left), 21, 28(left), 28(right), 43(lower right), back cover; Bill Lai, 16, 33(top), 42(top left); Stuart Cohen, 24(right); Rob Crandall, 26. *Index Stock*: Michele Burgess, 11(low); Lynn McLaren, 20. SuperStock: age fotostock, 12; Holton Collection, 14(low). *Robert Stock*: A. Jackamets, 13. *Art Resource, New York*: Jorge Ianiszewski, 15. *Envision*: Steven Needham, 22. *Andres Morya Photography*: 32(low), 36(top). *Magnum Photos*: Thomas Hoepker, 39; Sergio Larrain, 45.

Cover: *Cuernos del Paine and Lake Pehoe, Torres del Paine National Park, Chile*; Title page: *Quechua man*

Map and illustrations by Ian Warpole
Book design by Virginia Pope

Printed in Malaysia
1 3 5 6 4 2

Turn the Pages...

Where in the World Is Chile?

Chile is a land of variety. Dry deserts, snow-capped mountains, sandy beaches, and thick *temperate* rain forests fill the landscape of this South American country.

An Andean condor in flight

Chile snakes down the edge of the continent of South America like a long, skinny ribbon. The country is more than ten times longer than it is wide. In the north, it shares a small border with Peru. The neighboring countries of Bolivia and Argentina lie to the east. Its western edge borders the Pacific Ocean. Chile's coastline is almost 4,000 miles (6,435 kilometers) long, and Chile is the longest north-to-south country in the world.

Imagine you are an Andean condor, the national bird of Chile.

Chuquicamata, the world's largest open-pit copper mine, lies in the Atacama Desert.

Map of Chile

World map—Chile in red

Easter
Island
←

Pacific Ocean

0   300
Miles

KEY

☆ Capital city   River

● City   Mountain range

--- Border

PERU

BOLIVIA

BRAZIL

PARAGUAY

Arica ●

Atacama Desert

Norte
Grande

Aconcagua
River

ARGENTINA

URUGUAY

Valparaiso ● ☆ Santiago

Juan Fernández
Islands

Valle Central

Bío-Bío
River

Andes Mountains

Chiloé
Island

Atlantic Ocean

N
NW   NE
W   E
SW   SE
S

Strait of
Magellan

Cape
Horn

ANTARCTICA

A guanaco family

Flying from north to south, you would first fly over the Atacama Desert, one of the driest places on the globe. The world's largest open-pit copper mine, the Chuquicamata, lies in the Atacama Desert. Chile is the largest producer of copper in the world, which it trades with other countries.

Flying near the eastern and western borders of Chile, you would see that mountains line both sides of the country. The high Andes Mountains run along Chile's eastern border. Lower coastal mountains lie along the shoreline. The Andes are covered with snow much of the year. These mountains sometimes shake with earthquakes. Some are active volcanoes. In the mountains, you might see llamas, alpacas, vicuñas, and guanacos—all types of South American camels. Small chinchillas might be scurrying among the rocks. Rheas, large birds that do not fly, also live here.

Between the two mountain ranges lies a very fertile

The Bío-Bío River

Santiago, Chile

valley, called the Central Valley, or *Valle Central*. The soil in this area is very rich because of the water and *sediments* flowing down rivers that run from the Andes Mountains toward the sea, such as the Aconcagua and the Bío-Bío. Chileans grow crops in this soil. Vineyards produce grapes that are made into wine, and farms produce a wide variety of grains and fruits for *export*.

Chile's capital city, Santiago, is also in the Valle Central. Here, it is sunny and dry in summer, and rainy and cooler in winter. Summer lasts from December to March, and temperatures are about 70 degrees Fahrenheit (21 degrees Celsius). In winter, from June to September, temperatures are a little cooler, about 46 °F (8 °C).

A condor's view of southern Chile would show land thick with temperate rain forests and beautiful lakes. This part of Chile is cold and rainy. Some parts get up to 200 inches (500 centimeters) of rain a year. Farther south, the land gets rough and rocky with cold *glaciers*. Chile breaks apart into many islands in the south. This forms an *archipelago*. The southernmost tip of the country is called Cape Horn.

A glacier in Torres del Paine National Park

Chiloé Island lies close to the shore. Chile also owns several small islands farther out in the Pacific Ocean, including Easter Island and the Juan Fernández Islands. A triangle-shaped section of Antarctica, the cold, glacier-covered continent at the South Pole, is also claimed by Chile, although this is disputed by other countries.

Chiloé Island

The Atacama Desert

In the Great North of Chile, or the *Norte Grande*, lies the Atacama Desert. It is one of the driest places in the entire world. In some places in the Atacama it has never rained. Because it is so dry, few plants or animals can live here. However, some *oases*, or small patches of green, dot the landscape. Some parts of the Atacama, such as the Valley of the Moon, look like another planet, with tall craggy formations of salt and rock.

What Makes Chile Chilean?

Long ago, Chile was filled with native peoples, such as the Mapuche Indians. In the sixteenth century, *conquistadores* (soldiers from Spain) searched South America for gold. When the Spaniards came, the Indians tried to fight them off.

A Mapuche girl in traditional dress

They were not successful, and the Spaniards took over. Some native groups still thrive and maintain some of their old ways. Most of Chile, however, adopted the culture and traditions of Spain.

The Spanish people and Indian groups mixed. Today, there are about 16 million people living in Chile. Of that number, 95 percent are *mestizos* (people of mixed Spanish and Indian heritage) or European. Less than 5 percent are Indian. The largest Indian group is the Mapuche.

A Chilean teenager

Chilean people speak Spanish. Some of the native Indian cultures still speak their own languages, such as Mapudungu by the Mapuches and Rapanui by the residents of Easter Island. Also like Spain, most people in Chile (almost 90 percent) are Roman Catholic. Some groups are Protestant or other religions.

Chile's government has gone through many changes. In 1973, a military *dictator* named Augusto Pinochet took over the government. He jailed, killed, or drove away

This wooden church on Chiloé Island (left)
and this cathedral in Santiago (below) are places of prayer for Chileans.

La Moneda, the presidential palace in Santiago, Chile

people who did not agree with him. The people wanted more of a voice in their government, and during the 1980s, Pinochet allowed more freedoms, including some political activity. In 1989, Chileans refused Pinochet another eight-year term, and elected Patricio Aylwin. President Aylwin served from 1990 to 1994, in what was considered a transition period. Chile became a *democracy*. In January of 2006, Chileans elected the country's first woman president, Michelle Bachelet, who had once been put in prison under Pinochet's rule.

People enjoy art and music throughout Chile. In the city, one might go to a concert of the Chilean National Symphonic Orchestra. The National Ballet and other groups perform dance and opera. People can view art, such as paintings by Roberto Matta or others from Chile and around the world, at the Museum of Contemporary Art or the Museum of Fine Arts.

Literature has always been important to Chileans. Literature connects Chileans to their past and to the rest of the world. Two great poets recognized for their achievements are from Chile. Both Pablo Neruda and Gabriela Mistral won Nobel Prizes for their poetry. Isabel Allende is a famous novelist who is read not only in Chile, but all over the world. The National Library of Chile, in Santiago, is one of the oldest libraries in South America.

Traditional crafts of Chile are cherished by the people. At a *feria artesanal*, or craft fair, one might see weavings of llama and sheep's wool. Artists make colorful ponchos, blankets, and rugs. While most people in Chile dress as people do in the United States, some Mapuche women still wear bright shawls with large silver jewelry. Items are also made from copper, as well as lapis lazuli, a bright blue and very rare stone. Other natural items, such as cactus wood, are made into instruments. The Mapuche people also

A close-up of a colorful handwoven blanket

make instruments, such as *zamponas* (pan flutes) and *kultrunes* (drums), that are used for special ceremonies.

Music fills the air throughout the country. Folk songs, or *tonadas*, are popular. These poetic, often sad, tunes are sung to the music of a guitar.

A Mapuche man plays a traditional drum.

Chilean folk musicians

Arpilleras

A traditional craft of Chile is the making of *arpilleras*. Arpilleras are
story cloths. Women sew scraps of fabric onto burlap or stiff wool. These colorful pictures may take up to a year to make. The stories might be simple, such
as a picture of a farmer tending his crops, or scenes from Chilean folklore.

In Chile's history, arpilleras played an important role in politics. During the six-
teen years Pinochet ruled, he was cruel and unfair. Women sewed scenes of
the harsh treatment by soldiers and injustices against the people into
their arpilleras. The cloths helped to spread the word through
Chile, and people worked together for peace in
the country.

Living in Chile

More than 90 percent of the people in Chile live in the central valley. Businesses and the government are based in cities here, and crops are grown on its fertile land.

Santiago, the capital, is filled with the most activity. The city is packed with large skyscrapers and *plazas*, or public squares. Here, Chileans spend the day as people do in many other cities across the world. They work at restaurants, shops, or for the government or other businesses and factories.

The business district in Santiago, Chile

Houses in a poor neighborhood

People live in apartments or just outside the city in homes with gardens. Just as in many cities, there are wealthy areas and poor ones as well. In Santiago, many poor people live in neighborhoods called *poblaciones*.

A farmworker in a peach orchard

Life in the countryside is much different. For farmers, days are busy tending to crops. About 8 percent of Chileans are farmers or fishermen. Farmers grow wheat and corn, tomatoes, peaches, plums, apples, grapes, or sugar beets, as well as many other crops. Raising livestock is also a job of the rural Chilean. In the north, ranchers herd llamas or alpacas. In the south, there are cattle and sheep. In rural areas, night entertainment is not as glamorous as in the city. Men might play *cacho*, a dice game, while the women prepare the house for the next day. Children help their parents with the many chores that need to be done.

Shepherds guide their sheep through a town in the countryside.

Boats float near houses on stilts in a fishing village.

In some parts of the country, rural families might live in a house of *adobe*. In island areas, they might live in a house lifted up on stilts beside the shore.

In the very far south, the Mapuche people live as they have for thousands of years in the temperate rain forest, separated from the rest of the Chilean people. Their traditional homes, called *rukas*, look like haystacks.

Meals are central to any Chilean day. Breakfast is usually quick and easy, such as toast and tea or coffee. For lunch, or *almuerzo*, some stores and businesses close their doors, and some people return home for this meal between 1 p.m. and 3 p.m. This is the biggest meal of the day, with many courses and dessert. Later in the afternoon, between 5 p.m. and 7 p.m., families have *onces*. This evening snack might consist of a sandwich or a sweet dessert and tea. The fourth meal of the day is eaten after 9 p.m.

The cuisine of Chile is a mix of many cultures—Indian and Spanish, as well as other European cultures that have settled in Chile, such as German, French, and English.

Many Chilean dishes include potatoes or beans.

Seafood for sale at a fish market

21

Wine and bread, such as a thick bread called *pan amasado*, also accompanies most meals. Meat plays an important role in Chilean cooking. *Asados*, or barbeques, are a fun and common way to serve meat. Meat is also mixed with vegetables to make soups. Corn, tomatoes, and red peppers are common vegetables. *Pastel de choclo* is a baked corn casserole filled with meat and vegetables.

Because of Chile's long coastline and large fishing industry, seafood has become an important part of many Chilean recipes. The seafood market displays many choices. Lobster, crab, salmon, and sea bass are widely eaten. There are also clams, mussels, scallops, sea urchins, and even eels. *Caldillo* is a soup made from eel. *Paila marina* is a stew filled with all sorts of shellfish.

When it is time for a snack, *empanadas* are the most popular choice. They are pockets of pastry filled with meat, cheese, or seafood. They are sold at stands along the street and during festivals. They are easy to carry around and can be eaten on the go. They might also be the first course of a lunch meal.

Another fun snack food available on the go is a hot dog. On top of this treat, Chileans pile mayonnaise and ketchup, as well as *guacamole* (a sauce made from avocados).

Empanadas

Empanadas
(Meat Turnovers)

Ingredients:

For the dough

1 cup white flour

1 cup wheat flour

$1/2$ tablespoon baking powder

$1/2$ teaspoon salt

1 beaten egg

$3/4$ cup warm milk

$1/4$ cup olive oil

For the filling

1 tablespoon olive oil

$1/2$ teaspoon paprika

1 large onion

$1/4$ teaspoon chili powder

$1/4$ teaspoon cumin

$1/2$ pound ground beef

1 hard boiled egg

$1/4$ cup sliced black olives

$1/4$ cup raisins

Wash your hands before you begin. To make the dough, stir together flours, baking powder, and salt. Then add the egg, milk, and olive oil. Mix with a spatula until it is a stiff dough. Put it on a flat surface covered with flour, and knead about ten times. Divide it into eight balls and set aside.

Ask an adult to help you make the filling. Heat oil in a frying pan and add onions and paprika. Cook the onions about 5 to 10 minutes until they are soft. Add the meat, chili powder, and cumin. Cook about 5 to 10 more minutes until the meat is brown.

Roll out the eight pieces of dough into thin circles. Place a spoonful of filling onto each circle. Lay slices of egg, olives, and raisins on top.

Wet the edges of the circle with milk or water. Fold the dough to make a half-circle. Fold the ends over and flatten with a fork to seal the meat inside.

Place on a cookie sheet. Prick the top of each empanada twice with a fork. Cook in a 400 °F oven for 25–30 minutes until brown. Serve with tomato salsa. Makes eight empanadas.

School Days

Two girls on their way to school

Most people in Chile can read and write. Education is public, which means it is paid for by the government. All children must go to school through twelfth grade. There are also private schools, such as Catholic schools, where parents pay for their children to attend.

The school year lasts from March to December. Children get the summer months, January and February, off for vacation. Most schoolchildren wear uniforms of white shirts and blue jumpers for girls and white shirts, gray pants, and blue jackets for boys. In class, they learn Spanish, English, writing, science, history, and math.

Chile's history is an important part of school lessons. Children might learn about the mummies found high in the Andes that have given scientists clues about Chile's earliest people. They might learn about their native ancestors who lived off the land by herding and farming. They might try to uncap the

High school boys in their uniforms

Students and professors from the University of Chile do research on Easter Island.

mysteries behind the geoglyphs, or large murals, carved into sand dunes in the Norte Grande, to see what secrets they will reveal about Chile's past.

After high school, students have many choices. They can go to a technical or vocational school, where they will learn about computers, agriculture, or mining. Others might attend a university. There are many universities in Chile. Two popular ones are the University of Chile and the Pontifícia Universidad Católica de Chile. Here they will prepare for professional jobs, such as doctors, researchers, lawyers, or businesspeople. Some students with creative skills might attend the University

The University of Chile

of Chile's School of Art. Those who love music might attend the University of Chile's School of Music or the School of Ballet of Santiago's Municipal Theater, a school of dance.

Remembering traditions is part of children's education as well. On Easter Island there is one school where teachers work hard to teach the children their native language. On Chiloé Island in southern Chile, traditional myths are handed down from older people to the children so that the stories will always be remembered. Some of the characters from these myths include Trauco, a *satyr* of the forest; Pincoya, a beautiful maiden of the sea; or the Caleuche, a ghost ship feared by fishermen who head out in foggy weather.

La Araucana

One of the most important poems that Chilean children might learn in school is also a lesson in Chilean history. *La Araucana* was written by Alonso de Ercilla y Zúñiga (1533–1595). Ercilla was a Spanish soldier and poet who went to Chile in 1555 to fight the Indians there. He was inspired to write the poem when he saw the strength of Indian fighters who defended their land. The title of the poem refers to a Mapuche fighter named Lautaro who attacked and won battles against the Spanish.

Just for Fun

When Chileans relax, there are many things they can find to do in their country. In their free time, they might talk on cell phones or surf the Internet. In the city, they might run daily errands to the *supermercado* (supermarket) or visit the shops at the mall. They might take the subway, buses, or taxis to their destinations. They might

Teenagers at the mall

Shopping near the Plaza de Armas in the center of Santiago

People swim in the ocean and sit on the beach at Viña del Mar.

go to plays, operas, or the movies, or eat out at restaurants. They might hang out in the Plaza de Armas in the center of Santiago, where children might have a treat of cotton candy.

It is easy to move around the country. Chileans can take a boat from port to port, drive across the country on highways, or fly by plane.

In the summer, going to the beach is a common pastime. Along the Pacific coast, there are resorts, such as Viña del Mar, where people relax in the sun and play in the waves. In these warm-weather places, people might also enjoy fishing or yachting.

A snowboarder speeds down a mountain in Chile.

For those who enjoy cooler weather, there is a lot to do in Chile. The Andes Mountains are a vacation spot for Chilean tourists. Here they ski on the snowy slopes, or do other mountain activities, such as hiking, climbing, mountain biking, or white-water rafting.

Another cold-weather destination is Antarctica. While a small group of researchers actually live there, most people just go there for a visit because the weather is very harsh and cold.

Chilean soccer players (in red) control the ball during a game.

Sports are a fun activity for fans to attend. Chileans enjoy tennis, volleyball, basketball, and horse racing. By far, the most popular sport is soccer, called *fútbol* by Chileans. Children start young, practicing in parks and backyards. Professional teams draw large crowds as they try to reach the international World Cup competition.

Another very popular and traditional sporting event is the rodeo. Rodeos are a time for celebration. People wear traditional dress, listen to music, dance, and enjoy food together. The corral, called the *media-luna*, is semicircular in shape with an open side. Chilean cowboys, called *huasos*, take turns in the ring, riding their horses and trying to pin a bull to a soft

Cowboys ride in a rodeo.

Huasos in colorful costumes

and padded section of the wall. Unlike other rodeos in other countries, the animals are not roped or ridden.

Huasos are a symbol of Chilean tradition. Still roaming the *pampas*, or plains, huasos are known for their humor and wisdom. The colorful costume of the huaso is a symbol of Chile and its tradition. He wears a hat with a wide brim and flat top that ties under his chin. Around his waist, he wears a colorful sash. He also wears a poncho called a *manta*. His lower legs are covered by fringed chaps, or leggings, made of leather. On his feet are heavy boots, stirrups, and silver spurs.

Easter Island

Easter Island attracts visitors because it is a place of great mystery. Covering the island are large sculptures called *moai*. They are huge faces carved from stone. Some are as large as 20 feet tall. No one knows how or why these sculptures were built by people of the past. Also on the island, people have found script called *Rongorongo*, carved on wooden boards. Even experts have not been able to figure out what these ancient messages mean.

Let's Celebrate!

The Chilean flag

September 18, 1810, is an important date in Chilean history. This was when a non-Spanish council was formed to govern the country. Before that, Chile had been a colony, or settlement, of Spain for about 300 years. Today, the government of Chile is a democracy. A president as well as congressmen and women are elected by the people.

National Day, celebrated on September 18 every year, is Chile's independence day. It is one of the country's most important and festive holidays. September is the beginning of spring, so everyone enjoys spending the day outdoors. Vendors sell pinwheels and flags for children to wave while they watch the parades of soldiers and bands. They eat grilled foods in outdoor asados.

Soldiers participate in a National Day celebration.

On National Day, kite flying is a popular activity and fills the sky with a colorful display. Traditionally, flying kites was a popular activity among priests. Today, both children and adults enjoy it. Sometimes people can get very competitive. *Bolas* are large hollow kites. People might try to snare a larger bola with a smaller, quicker kite and bring it down.

In parks and other public spaces, *fondas* are set up. These are tents held up by poles, where people can eat and dance together. Food and drink, such as a cider called *chichi*, are enjoyed by all.

Catholics parade in Santiago.

Men carry a cross during an
Easter procession.

Because the Catholic religion is important to Chileans, religious holy days are a time for celebration. Weddings and first communions are times for families to gather together. On saint days, people carrying religious statues parade the streets in cities and villages. Christmas and Easter are joyous events. On Christmas morning, children open presents left by *El Viejo Pasquero* (the old Christmas man) before going to the beach to celebrate.

La Tirana is one of the most popular religious festivals in Chile. La Tirana is a small village in northern Chile, near the Atacama Desert. In July each year, thousands of people gather for the festivities that last a week long. Dancing and music are a big part of the celebrations. Costumes are colorful and bright, and people dance late into the night for many days. The tunes from trumpets, whistles, cymbals, and drums fill the air. The visitors to La Tirana also attend mass at the church of the Virgin of Carmen.

Another festival held during the summer months is called *trilla a yeguas*. This celebrates the harvest of wheat, one of Chile's

A man dressed in a colorful mask and costume

most important crops. Huasos guide horses over the wheat. Their trampling sep-arates the grains of wheat from the unusable part, called the chaff. Harps and guitars play music, and everyone is in a festive mood.

Chileans are always looking for occasions to celebrate. They are proud of their culture, their history, their varied land, their good food, and the people of this beautiful country.

A couple dances during a celebration of the wheat harvest.

The Cueca

Celebrations in Chile are often not complete without dancing the *cueca*, the national dance of Chile. The dance is performed by a man and a woman, who move to the music of harps, tambourines, and accordions. The man and woman represent a rooster courting a hen. The dance gets faster and faster as the dancers wave their handkerchiefs in the air. The end of the dance is very noisy, as the dancers, and spectators, loudly stamp their feet.

The flag of Chile has three colors: white, red, and blue. These colors symbolize different things. The white represents the snow-capped Andes, the blue symbolizes the sky, and the red stands for the blood spilled in the struggle for independence. There are two horizontal bands, white on top and red on the bottom, and a blue square in the upper left corner that contains a white star, which represents a guide to progress and honor.

The Chilean form of money is called the peso. One hundred centavos make up one peso. In March 2006, one U.S. dollar equaled about 527 Chilean pesos.

Count in Spanish

English	Spanish	Say it like this:
one	uno	OO-noh
two	dos	dohs
three	tres	trace
four	cuatro	KWAH-troh
five	cinco	SEEN-koh
six	seis	sayss
seven	siete	see-EH-tay
eight	ocho	OH-choh
nine	nueve	NWEH-vay
ten	diez	dee-EHS

Glossary

adobe (uh-DOH-bee)   Bricks made from mud.

archipelago (ar-kuh-PUHL-ah-go)   A group or string of islands.

democracy (duh-MAK-ruh-see)   A government where the people elect the leaders.

dictator (DIK-tate-uhr)   A ruler who has absolute control.

export   Sharing and selling goods to another country.

glacier (GLAY-shuhr)   A large piece of moving ice that covers land.

oases (oh-AY-seez)   Areas of vegetation in an otherwise dry and empty desert.

satyr (SAY-tuhr)   An imaginary creature that is part man and part horse or goat.

sediments   The soil and other material carried by a river.

temperate   An area that has lots of rain and trees, and mild temperatures.

Fast Facts

Chile snakes down the edge of the continent of South America. The country is more than ten times longer than it is wide. Chile's coastline is almost 4,000 miles (6,435 km) long. It is the longest north-to-south country in the world.

Arica

Atacama Desert

Norte Grande

Aconcagua River

Valparaiso ● ★Santiago

Juan Fernández Islands

Bío-Bío River

Valle Central

Andes Mountains

Chiloé Island

Strait of Magellan

Cape Horn

The high Andes Mountains run along Chile's eastern border. The Andes are covered with snow much of the year.

Chile's capital city, Santiago, is in the Valle Central. More than 90 percent of the people in Chile live in the central valley.

The Andean condor is the national bird of Chile.

Southern Chile is thick with temperate rain forests and beautiful lakes. This part of Chile is cold and rainy. Some parts get up to 200 inches (500 cm) of rain a year.

The flag of Chile has three colors: white, red, and blue. The white represents the snow-capped Andes, the blue symbolizes the sky, and the red stands for the blood spilled in the struggle for independence. The blue square in the upper left corner contains a white star, which represents a guide to progress and honor.

In Chile, 89 percent of the people are Roman Catholic and 11 percent are Protestant or other religions.

The Chilean form of money is called the peso. One hundred centavos make up one peso.

Chilean people speak Spanish. However, some of the native Indian cultures still speak their own languages.

The government of Chile is a democracy. A president as well as a congress are elected by the people.

Chile's Atacama Desert is one of the driest places on the globe. The world's largest open-pit copper mine, the Chuquicamata, lies in the Atacama Desert. Chile is the largest producer of copper in the world.

As of July 2006, there were 16,134,219 people living in Chile. Of that number, 95 percent are mestizos or European. Less than 5 percent are Indian.

Proud to Be Chilean

Lautaro (1537–1556)

Lautaro was a chief among the Mapuche Indian people. When Spaniards took over Mapuche land, Lautaro was taken prisoner and made to work for them. But Lautaro escaped and returned to the side of his fellow Indians. He led fierce battles against the Spanish and became a hero to his people. Lautaro died in a surprise nighttime attack, but he will always be remembered. The historic poem *La Araucana* details his brave feats.

Pablo Neruda (1904–1973)

Pablo Neruda was a prize-winning Chilean poet. In 1971, he won the Nobel Prize in Literature, an international recognition of his work. He loved Chile and its people. Many of his poems describe Chile's beautiful landscape and the strength of its residents. His poems also spoke for the poor and factory workers who did not have a voice. Because some of his poetry criticized the government, he went into exile on Isla Negra, living in a famous house that is still visited by many today.

Violeta Parra (1917–1967)

Violeta Parra was a leading folk musician in Chile. Growing up in a home of storytellers and musicians, Violeta started to travel Chile, gathering stories and inspiration for her work. She loved to express the thoughts of the rural people of Chile, her love for her country, and her frustration with the government that did not always treat its people fairly. The songs she sang were like poems set to guitar music. Her creativity also went beyond song. She was a painter, sculptor, and sewed beautiful arpilleras.

Find Out More

Books

Enchantment of the World: Chile by Sylvia McNair. Children's Press, Danbury, Connecticut, 2000.

First Reports Countries: Chile by Cynthia Klingel and Robert B. Noyed. Compass Point Books, Minnesota, 2002.

Modern Nations of the World: Chile by David Schaffer. Lucent Books, 2004.

Web Sites*

www.chile-usa.org

This Web site is the official site of *The Embassy of Chile* and includes an overview of the country and its politics.

www.odci.gov/cia/publications/factbook/geos/ci.html

The World Factbook lists all the important facts about Chile, with information about the land, people, government, and business.

Videos

Gjerde, Barry. *Travel the World By Train: South America.* Pioneer Entertainment, 1999.

*All Internet sites were available and accurate when sent to press.

Index

Page numbers for illustrations are in **boldface.**

About the Author

Dana Meachen Rau is an author, editor, and illustrator. A graduate of Trinity College in Hartford, Connecticut, she has written more than one hundred books for children, including nonfiction, biographies, early readers, and historical fiction. She lives and works in Burlington, Connecticut, with her husband, Chris, and children, Charlie and Allison.

Acknowledgments

Special thanks to the Embassy of Chile, Cultural Department, in Washington, D.C., for their help in providing research.